My First — SHARED READING

I Can Read!

W9-BVG-777

TY'S TRAVELS
Lab Magic

by Kelly Starling Lyons   pictures by Nina Mata

HARPER

An Imprint of HarperCollinsPublishers

For Kairo and Messiah,
always remember that
magic lives in you
—K.S.L.

Dedicated to every curious,
imaginative mind—
make your own magic.
—N.M.

I Can Read® and I Can Read Book® are trademarks of HarperCollins Publishers.

Ty's Travels: Lab Magic

Text copyright © 2022 by Kelly Starling Lyons

Illustrations copyright © 2022 by Nina Mata

Library of Congress Control Number: 2021941903

ISBN 978-0-06-295117-5 (trade bdg.)—ISBN 978-0-06-295116-8 (pbk.)

Book design by Rachel Zegar

21 22 23 24 25   LSCC   10 9 8 7 6 5 4 3 2 1

❖

First Edition

Dear Parent:
Your child's love of reading starts here!

Every child learns to read in a different way and at his or her own speed. Some go back and forth between reading levels and read favorite books again and again. Others read through each level in order. You can help your young reader improve and become more confident by encouraging his or her own interests and abilities. From books your child reads with you to the first books he or she reads alone, there are I Can Read Books for every stage of reading:

SHARED READING
Basic language, word repetition, and whimsical illustrations, ideal for sharing with your emergent reader

BEGINNING READING
Short sentences, familiar words, and simple concepts for children eager to read on their own

READING WITH HELP
Engaging stories, longer sentences, and language play for developing readers

READING ALONE
Complex plots, challenging vocabulary, and high-interest topics for the independent reader

I Can Read Books have introduced children to the joy of reading since 1957. Featuring award-winning authors and illustrators and a fabulous cast of beloved characters, I Can Read Books set the standard for beginning readers.

A lifetime of discovery begins with the magical words **"I Can Read!"**

Visit www.icanread.com for information
on enriching your child's reading experience.

Ty jumps out of bed.

He wakes his brother, Corey.

"Get up! Get up!"

It's almost time to go.

Ty loves science.
Corey does, too.

They can't wait for Momma
to take them to the museum.

When Ty and Corey step
through the doors,
they are scientists.

Sometimes they study bugs.
Sometimes they catch the wind.

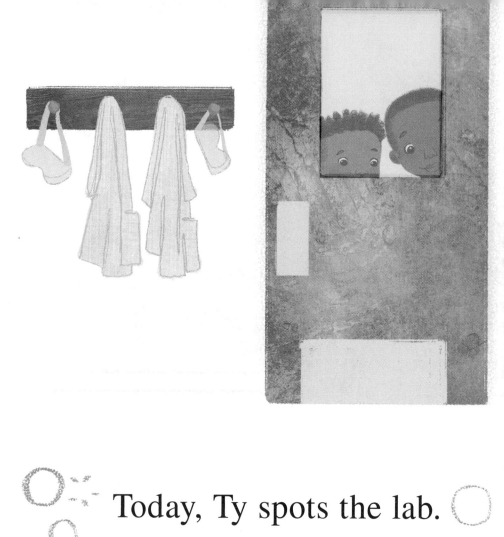

Today, Ty spots the lab.
He sees white coats
and goggles.

10

Ty sees test tubes.
He sees scientists
hard at work.

MUST BE 8 OR
OLDER TO
ENTER
SCIENCE LAB

Oh no! Momma sees a sign.

Ty is too little.

Momma hugs him.

"It's okay, Ty," Corey says.
Ty walks away slowly.

Momma, Corey, and Ty
visit the butterflies.
Wings flap and flutter.

Ty and Corey sit still.

A butterfly lands on Corey.

Ty smiles.

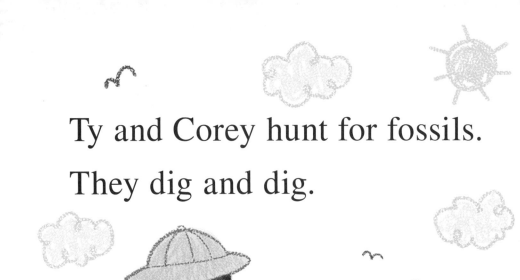

Ty and Corey hunt for fossils.

They dig and dig.

16

Ty finds a shark tooth.
Corey cheers.

The brothers sail boats
and steer with the wind.
"Amazing!" Momma says.

Ty sees the lab on the way out.
Now he knows what to do!

When he gets home,

Ty runs upstairs.

He puts on Dad's white shirt.

He puts on goggles.

Corey grins at Ty.

Momma gets out bowls
and cups.
Daddy sets up a table.

Ty and Corey walk
into their lab.

The scientists are hard at work.

They pour and mix.

They pull and stretch.

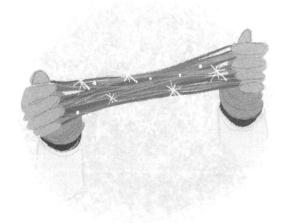

"Check it out," Ty says.

Next, Ty and Corey
make bubbles.
Then they blow them.

Momma and Daddy
catch them.
Pop!

Ty and Corey
test experiments.
Colors dance.
Water fizzes.

They help each other.

They discover new things.

Ty loves science.
Corey does, too.

At the museum and at home,
it's fun being scientists.

Together.